D0453442

Don't be Afraid, Little Ones

M Christina Butler
Caroline Pedler

LITTLE TIGER PRESS
London

Deep in the soft green shadows of the jungle
Mother Tiger watched over her tiny cubs.

The cubs grew strong as the days
passed by. Little Kai learned
how to pounce . . .

and Amber
learned to make
surprise attacks!

At the end of each day the cubs snuggled into the silky safety of their mother's side and fell asleep to the rumble of her purr.

Then one night Mother Tiger went hunting. "Wait for me here, my little ones," she said.

When she had gone, the night seemed bigger and darker, full of strange noises.

The cubs waited and waited. "She'll be back soon," said Amber.

But still Mother Tiger did not return.

"I do wish she'd come," whimpered Kai.

Amber stared anxiously into the darkness. "Let's go and find her," she said.

Through silver patterns of moonlight the cubs padded down the jungle pathway. Dark shapes and silent shadows followed them through the trees.

Then from
behind them
came a noise.

RUSTLE!
CRACKLE!
SWISH!

Amber gasped. "What's that?"

"I-I don't know," whispered Kai. "Is it a crocodile?"

They stared into the night, their eyes open wide, as the sound came closer.

RUSTLE!

CRACKLE!

SWISH!

"Run!" growled Amber. "Run as fast as you can!"

Crashing and bounding, faster and faster, the cubs raced through the grass.

"STOP!" cried Kai suddenly.

In front of them the river swirled dark and deep. The cubs could go no further, and the noise was getting nearer!

With their ears flat and their heads low, the cubs turned and stood together.

"We're not afraid of you!" they roared in their loudest, fiercest voices. "Even if you are a crocodile!"

The grasses rippled and snapped, then out stepped . . .

. . . Mother Tiger!

"We thought you'd left us!" Amber and Kai cried, leaping up to her.

Mother Tiger nuzzled her cubs. "You knew I'd come back," she purred. "Follow me, little ones . . ."

Deep in the soft shadows of the jungle Mother Tiger and her cubs snuggled together.

"I'm not afraid of crocodiles anyway," Kai told his mother bravely. "Are you, Amber?"

But Amber was fast asleep.

For our four little tigers, with love ~ M C B

To my friends and family, also to two little miracles, Jodie and Woody ~ C P

LITTLE TIGER PRESS
1 The Coda Centre, 189 Munster Road, London SW6 6AW
www.littletiger.co.uk

First published in Great Britain 2007
This edition published 2012

Text copyright © M Christina Butler 2007
Illustrations copyright © Caroline Pedler 2007
M Christina Butler and Caroline Pedler have asserted their rights to be identified as the author and illustrator of this work under the Copyright, Designs and Patents Act, 1988

All rights reserved

Printed in China • LTP/1800/0794/0413

4 6 8 10 9 7 5 3

Deep in the soft green shadows
of the jungle two tiny tiger cubs
pounce and play with their mother.
But then one night Mother Tiger goes into
the jungle to hunt. Left alone, the cubs
find the night seems much bigger
and darker than before . . .

This book is part of a set and
should not be sold separately.

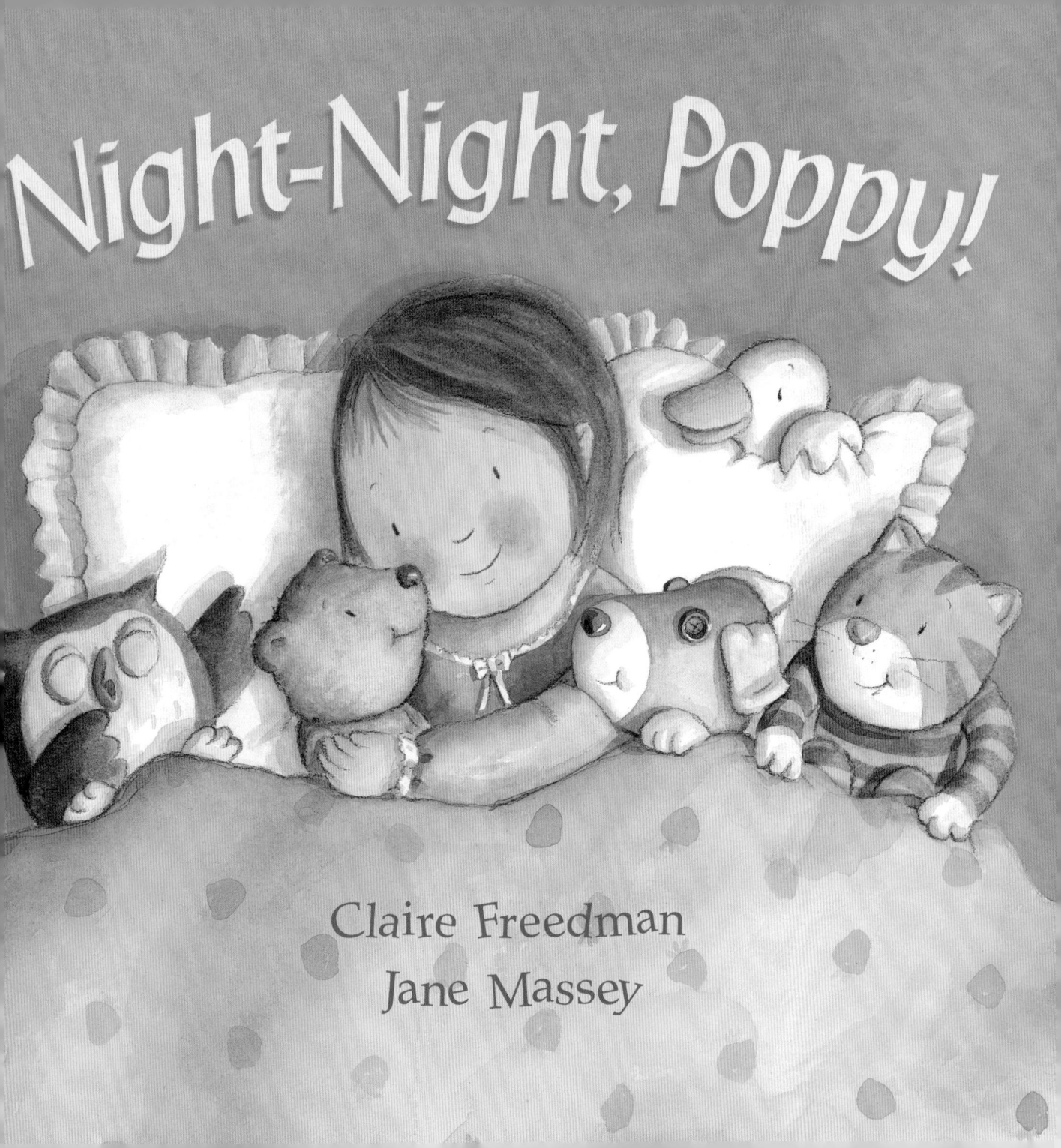
Night-Night, Poppy!
Claire Freedman
Jane Massey